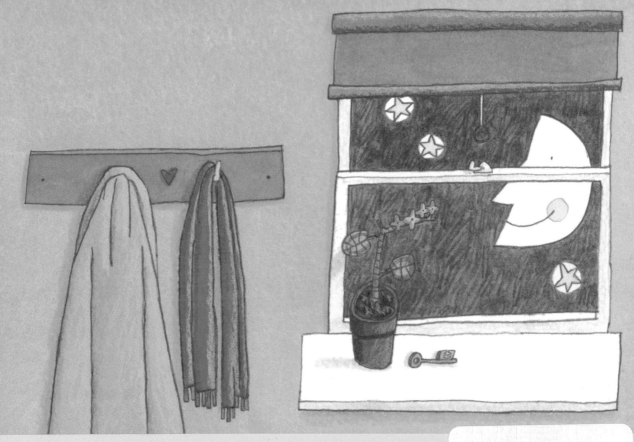

It is night.

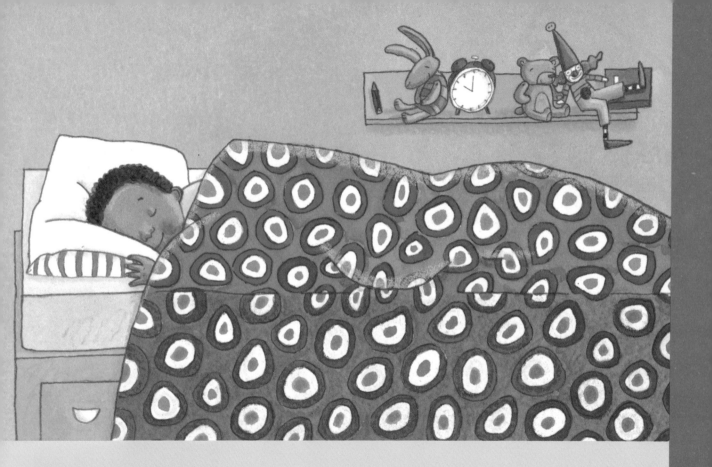

Sammy is sleeping.

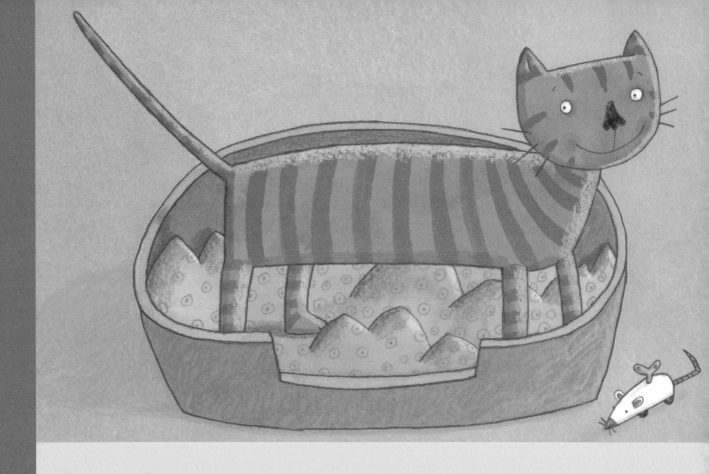

But Tabby Cat is awake.

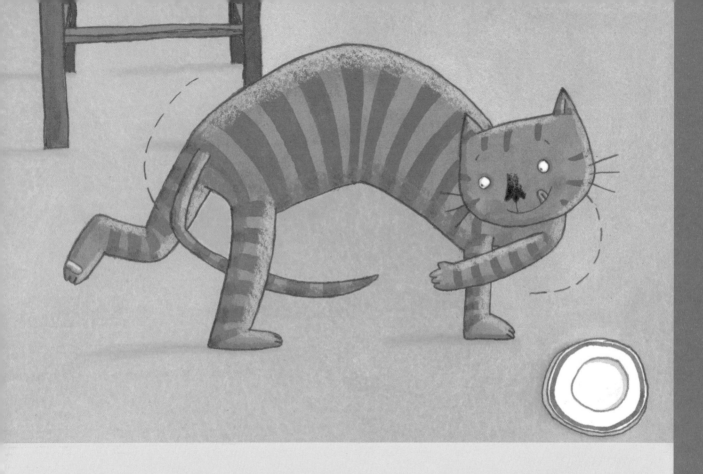

Tabby Cat plays with her tail.

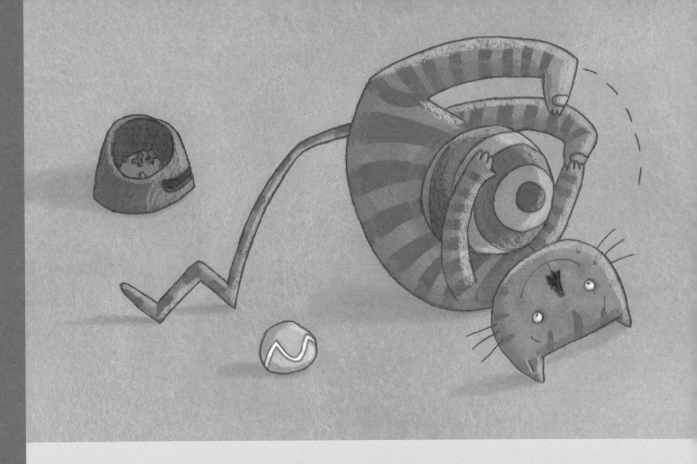

Tabby Cat plays with a ball.

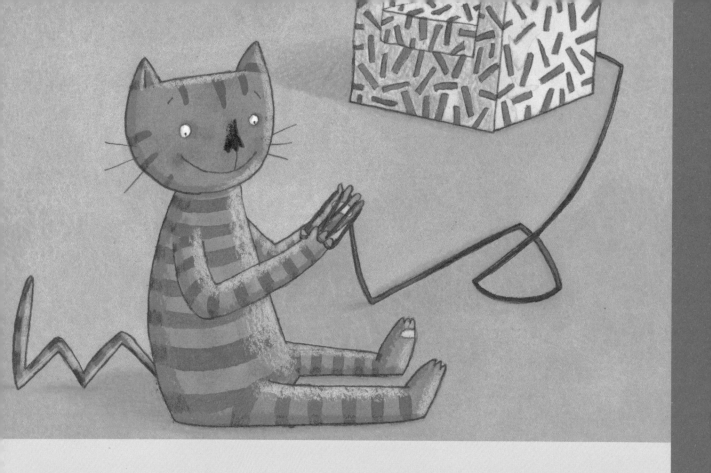

Tabby Cat plays with a string.

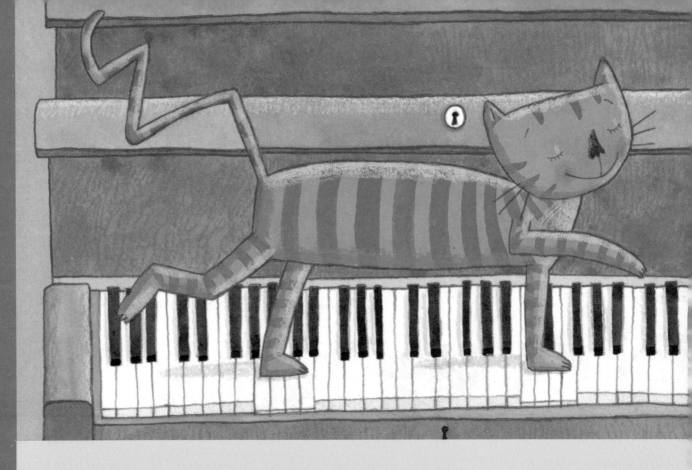

Tabby Cat plays with a piano.

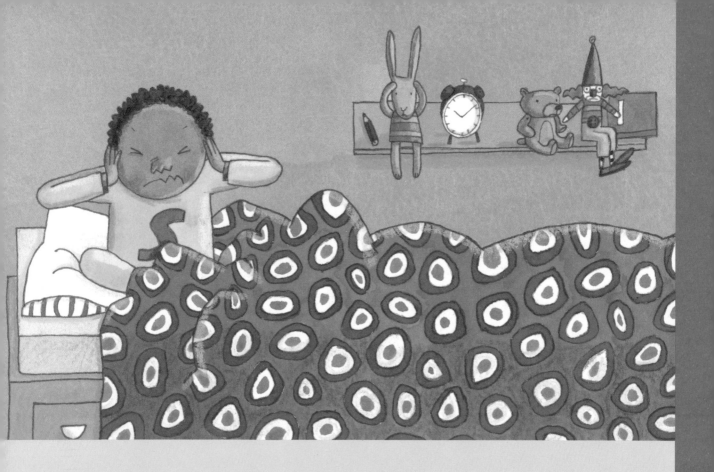

Now Sammy is awake!